THIS WALKER BOOK BELONGS TO:

For Banana Ted, from Banana Mummy x

First published 2020 by Walker Books Ltd, 87 Vauxhall Walk, London SE11 5HJ

10 9 8 7 6 5 4 3 2 1

© 2020 Yasmeen Ismail

The right of Yasmeen Ismail to be identified as author/illustrator of this work has been asserted by her in accordance with the Copyright, Designs and Patents Act 1988

This book has been typeset in Walbaum

Printed in China

British Library Cataloguing in Publication Data: a catalogue record for this book is available from the British Library

ISBN 978-1-4063-7584-8

www.walker.co.uk

Would You Like a BANANA?

Yasmeen Ismail

WALKER BOOKS
AND SUBSIDIARIES
LONDON • BOSTON • SYDNEY • AUCKLAND

I'm hungry.

Would you like a banana?

No. It's too yellow. It's too bendy.

It is too wonky.

I won't eat a banana.

But you might *like* a banana.

Just try a teeny taste.

Would you like one on a plate?

No.

No.

You might like one with some bread,

or maybe standing on your head.

I won't eat a banana.

What about a little one?

Or maybe one that's in a bun?

No. I won't

How about I eat one too,
is that something *we* can do?

No. I won't
BAN

You might like it in the end.

In a bowl?

With a friend?

No. I won't eat a banana.

Watch its yellow belly
wobble on a happy jelly.

Upside-down or right way up,
mash it in your favourite cup.

Bananas can be
good with honey.

Slice it up,
pretend it's money.

Pop a candle on
and make
a very special
birthday cake.

There are so
many ways how.
Would you like to
eat one now?

No. I won't eat a BANANA!
That's what I SAID!

I won't eat one with some bread,

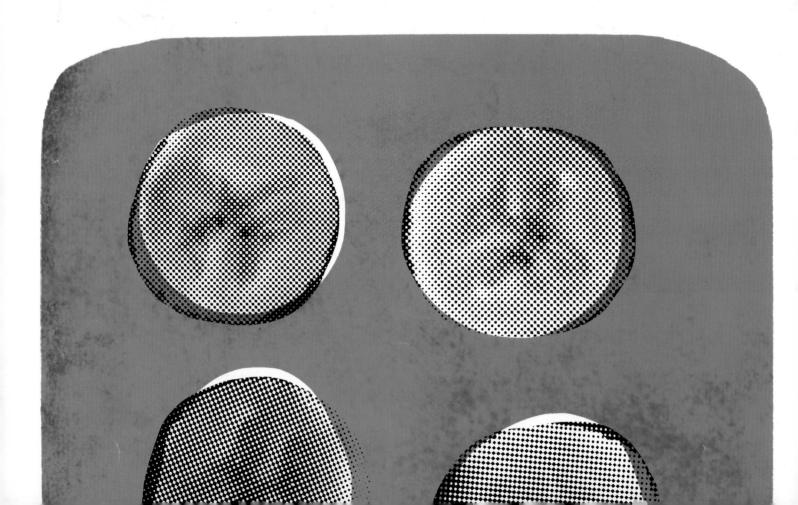

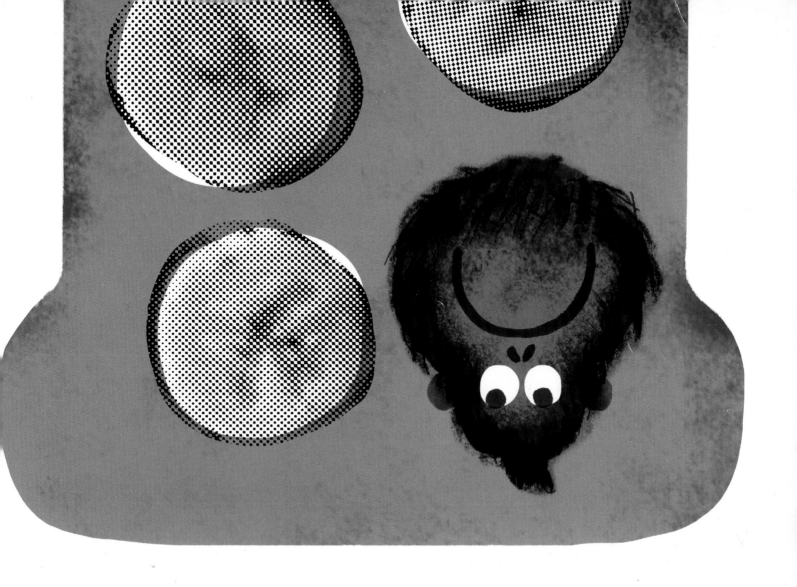

I won't eat one on my head.

I won't eat one up and down,

inside - outside,
right-side, wrong-side,

round the bend,

in the end,
up and under,

I won't

eat a banana.

OK.

You don't have to eat a banana.

HEY!

Where's the banana?

I want another banana.

Say please.

Banana Split